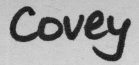

Tales of
Action and
Suspense

by
Debra Weiss

Watermill Press

Covey

Contents of this edition copyright © 1983 by Watermill
Press, Mahwah, New Jersey

Printed in the United States of America

Illustrations by Thomas Heggie

ISBN 0-89375-803-5

Contents

Where's Cathy?

Jenny Andrews sighed as she finished the book. *It's so romantic!* she thought as she stared ahead dreamily. She imagined herself as Miranda Shane, the daring heroine of the book. Miranda was a world-famous detective. She had a different disguise for each day of the year.

Jenny drifted out of her fantasy world. She felt distracted all of a sudden. It was too quiet in the room.

"Cathy?" Jenny called out. She turned around to see what her baby sister was up to. Cathy was two years old and had a bad habit of getting into trouble the minute Jenny turned her back. Jenny didn't see Cathy anywhere.

Oh, no, she thought. *I never should have let her out of my sight. I'm really going to get it if she gets into Mom's make-up again!*

Jenny ran up the stairs to her parents' room. Ever since Cathy had learned to climb the stairs, she'd been a real problem to look after. The last time Jenny baby-sat for her, Cathy spilled half a bottle of chocolate syrup on the kitchen floor before Jenny could stop her.

"Cathy! Where are you? Oh, Cathy!"

Jenny was beginning to get worried.

Jenny was beginning to get worried. She'd opened every door and looked in every room upstairs. But Cathy was so little, she could hide almost anywhere.

Jenny went back downstairs and searched the kitchen and dining room. She looked behind the coats in the hall closet.

"Cathy, are you hiding? I give up. I can't find you. Come on out, now," Jenny pleaded. But Cathy didn't come out. Jenny was really nervous now. *She must have gotten outside,* she thought. *But how could she have moved that heavy door all by herself?*

Jenny ran to the front door and saw that it was locked and bolted. But when she checked the back door, she groaned. It was halfway open. And Cathy's rubber duck was lying in the doorway.

Jenny grabbed the house keys and

went after Cathy. *She couldn't have gone far,* Jenny said to herself. Jenny searched carefully in the garden, the backyard, and all around the outside of the house. Her calls attracted the attention of Mr. Gotham, the Andrews' next-door neighbor. He was outside trimming some bushes.

"What's the matter? Are you looking for the little one?" he asked.

"Yes. I was reading, and when I looked up, she was gone. I've searched the whole house for her," Jenny said all in one breath.

"I see," Mr. Gotham said thoughtfully. "Well, don't worry. She can't be very far away. You just calm down, and everything will be fine. I'll take this side of the street and you take the other, O.K.? We'll find her soon."

"Oh, thank you, Mr. Gotham," Jenny

9

said, close to tears. She crossed the street and began to comb the block for Cathy. There were only three houses and an empty lot on the dead-end street. She looked in the yards, behind all the trees and bushes. She looked over at Mr. Gotham. There was still no sign of Cathy.

As she crossed the street to talk to Mr. Gotham, Jenny swallowed hard. She had a terrible lump in her throat. Maybe Cathy had been kidnapped! Jenny had read a lot of stories about that sort of thing. How would she ever find her? Or maybe Cathy had been in an accident. She might be in the hospital this very minute! But which hospital?

As Jenny reached Mr. Gotham, she broke down and started sobbing. "Oh, where's Cathy?" she asked through her tears. "I'm sure something terrible has happened, and it's all my fault!"

"Now, now, Jenny," Mr. Gotham said gently. "I'm sure nothing terrible has happened. But we do have a problem. I think we need some help. Where are your parents?"

"They're on their way to Glen Lake to visit some friends," Jenny replied. "They left here at 4:00." Mr. Gotham looked at his watch. The Andrews wouldn't be in Glen Lake for another hour.

"I see," he said as he looked at Jenny's worried face. "I think we ought to call the police," he suggested. He didn't want to alarm Jenny, but he was beginning to get worried himself. Where could Cathy have gone?

Jenny and Mr. Gotham went back to the Andrews' house. Mr. Gotham called the local police.

"Yes, yes . . . of course," Mr. Gotham

was saying. He turned to Jenny. "The police would like a description of Cathy." He handed her the phone.

Jenny took the receiver with a trembling hand. A policeman asked her Cathy's age, hair color, and height. He wanted to know what clothes Cathy was wearing when she was last seen.

When Jenny finished describing her little sister, there was a pause. She could hear her heart pounding. Finally, the policeman cleared his throat and said, "Just sit tight, young lady. We'll send a detective over right away."

The policeman hung up before Jenny could say anything more. *A detective!* she thought to herself. She wondered if the detective would look like Miranda Shane. Then she got angry at herself again. If she hadn't been so busy thinking about Miranda Shane in the first place, this never would have happened!

The doorbell rang and Jenny jumped up to answer it. A kind-looking, fair-haired man in gray stood in the doorway. Jenny looked at him with disappointment. He reminded her of her math teacher, Mr. Thompson.

"Bill Carlin, police," the man said, showing her his I.D. "Is this the Andrews residence?"

"Yes, it is," said Mr. Gotham, coming up behind Jenny. "Won't you come in?"

After a brief discussion, Jenny, Mr. Gotham, and Mr. Carlin went outside to begin their search for Cathy. "How long have you lived in this neighborhood?" Mr. Carlin asked Jenny.

"Since I was a baby," Jenny replied.

"Have any new folks moved in here lately?" he asked.

"No...everybody on this block has

13

*"Bill Carlin, police," the man said, showing
Jenny his I.D.*

lived here for about as long as I can remember."

"I've lived here for twenty-five years," Mr. Gotham said. "This is a peaceful, friendly neighborhood. Everybody knows each other."

Mr. Carlin frowned. "Before we question anybody, I want to take a look around," he said. Jenny and Mr. Gotham followed Mr. Carlin as he walked down the block. He stooped down all of a sudden, and Jenny almost tripped over him.

"A fresh footprint," Mr. Carlin said. He pointed to a tiny print of a baby's shoe in the soil.

"That's Cathy's footprint. I'm sure of it!" Jenny said excitedly.

Mr. Carlin continued up the footpath toward a big house. Then he came to another sudden stop. "Excuse me," Mr.

Gotham said, as he bumped into Mr. Carlin.

"What is it?" Jenny asked eagerly.

Mr. Carlin reached into a lilac bush and pulled out a dirty pink ribbon.

"That's Cathy's ribbon! She was wearing it today!" Jenny exclaimed.

"Who lives in this house?" Mr. Carlin asked as he walked toward the front door.

"This is the Grandys' house," Mr. Gotham said. "Harold and Sally Grandy, their two kids, and Mrs. Grandy's mother. They've lived here for years."

There was a long silence after Mr. Carlin rang the doorbell. Jenny held her breath.

Finally, the door opened up a crack and a pair of kindly blue eyes peeped out. It opened a few inches more, and a very tiny, very old lady in a strange-looking dress stood in the doorway.

"I know, you've come to join the party," she said with a smile. "You must forgive me, but I've forgotten your names. My memory's a little rusty these days. Do come in," she added.

Mr. Gotham whispered in Mr. Carlin's ear as they all entered the house.

"Is Cathy here, Mrs. McGee?" Jenny asked loudly. She knew that Mrs. Grandy's mother was very deaf.

"You must mean Samantha, dear," she corrected Jenny. "It's her birthday today," Mrs. McGee explained.

Mr. Carlin gave Mr. Gotham a wink. "Of course, that's why we're here. Now won't you take us in to see her?" he asked Mrs. McGee.

"Cathy!" Jenny exclaimed, as she caught sight of her baby sister eating a big piece of chocolate cake. Cathy was wearing a party hat and grinning from

*Cathy was wearing a party hat and grinning
from ear to ear.*

ear to ear.

"Chocky?" she asked Jenny, offering her a piece of cake.

"Oh, Cathy, you gave me such a scare!" Jenny said as she threw her arms around her baby sister.

"Well, you won't need me anymore," Mr. Carlin said. "Are you all right now, young lady?" he asked Jenny.

"I'm fine, thanks to you," Jenny said with relief. "Oh, Mr. Carlin. . .," Jenny paused for a moment. "You won't tell my parents about this, will you?"

"I don't see any reason to get them all upset, do you?" he asked with a smile.

"Gee, thanks for everything," Jenny said, shaking his hand.

"Won't you all sit down?" Mrs. McGee asked. "The ice cream is beginning to melt."

River of Gold

As Jimmy piled more chicken on his plate, his sister Marsha made a face. "Boy, can you ever eat!" she said. "What's that, your third helping?"

"Fourth," Jimmy said, biting into a drumstick.

"It's nice to see someone who appreciates your mother's cooking," Mr. Green said. He looked at Marsha's plateful of untouched food.

Marsha frowned. "I'm on a diet. I wish I could eat like the bottomless pit over there," she said, pointing to Jimmy.

"That's enough, you two," Mrs. Green said. She looked at her husband. "John, you were saying something about a gold deal?"

"Gold deal—wow!" exclaimed Jimmy.

"Yeah, tell us, Dad!" added Marsha.

"Just hold on, everybody, and I'll tell you what happened," Mr. Green said, settling back in his chair.

"I ran into Ralph Bradley, the real estate man, at the bank today," he began. "Ralph was all excited about this 'river of gold' thirty miles west of here, up in the mountains," Mr. Green said.

"A river of gold?" Mrs. Green asked.

"A river of gold?" Mrs. Green asked.

"Yes. Ralph said he's never seen anything like it. A Mr. Jake Parker discovered gold in one of those mountain streams near Millerstown."

"And who is Jake Parker?" Mrs. Green asked.

"He's a gold prospector from California. I met him—he is quite a man! Why, he has struck gold twenty times in the last ten years!" Mr. Green said.

Mrs. Green sighed. "So Ralph talked you into investing some money in this so-called river of gold?" she asked.

"Nobody talked me into anything," Mr. Green said, frowning, "but I did decide to buy a claim in the river."

"You mean you're going to pan for gold?" Marsha asked excitedly.

"That's right," Mr. Green said.

"Can we try, too?" Jimmy asked him,

laying down his fork for the first time.

"Sure, why not?" Mr. Green smiled. "The more, the merrier. We can pretend we're back in the days of the Old West."

"John, how much did this claim cost?" Mrs. Green asked.

"Oh, it was a good deal. Ralph gave me a break since he's a friend." Mr. Green cleared his throat. "It was only $3,000."

"Three thousand!" Mrs. Green said. "What about the repairs on the stables, John? How are we going to pay for them?" she asked angrily.

"Don't worry, Ann. We'll make the money back in no time. Ralph was the first to stake a claim, and you should see the size of the gold nuggets he found in just one week! Besides, the Brewers and the Carsons have bought claims in the river, and they're no fools. This deal is legitimate, believe me."

"I hope so," Mrs. Green said, "but I sure would like to see this river for myself."

"Oh, you will—next Sunday, when the river officially opens up for gold panning. Ralph's helping Parker and his men set things up this week."

"I can't wait!" Marsha said. "By the way, Dad, where is this river?"

"It's about two miles north of Pilgrim's Pass, in the middle of thick forest land. It's such rough country, you can only reach it by horse. Yes, sir, this is going to be a real adventure," Mr. Green chuckled.

"I don't like the sound of it," Mrs. Green said, shaking her head.

The next morning, Marsha was up before dawn. She couldn't get the river of gold out of her mind. She decided to go see it for herself. She put on her robe and slipped quietly into the kitchen. To her surprise, Jimmy was sitting at the kitchen table, looking at a map.

"I couldn't sleep," she whispered. "I kept thinking about the river of gold."

"Me, too," Jimmy said. "Why don't we go there today?"

"Great! There's only a half-day of school, so we can get an early start."

As soon as school let out, Marsha and Jimmy hurried home, dropped off their books, and went outside to saddle up the horses. Soon, they were ready to go.

As they rode across the field toward Harper's Trail, Jimmy whooped and burst into a gallop. Marsha caught up with him and they raced to the trail.

"A dead heat!" Jimmy yelled, as they finished neck and neck.

Marsha and Jimmy rode along the

Jimmy was sitting at the kitchen table,
looking at a map.

trail for about an hour. They were climbing steadily toward Pilgrim's Pass, making good time because the ground was firm and smooth. As they approached the pass, the trail got very steep and rocky.

When they finally reached the pass, they looked out over the blue-green mountains.

"We're really getting close now," said Marsha. "Dad said the river was two miles to the north."

Harper's Trail ended at Pilgrim's Pass. Other smaller trails branched off to the south and west. To the north, there was no trail at all—just rocky, uneven ground covered with trees and brush.

Marsha and Jimmy led the horses slowly between the trees and bushes. After a mile, the forest was so thick that they had to dismount and lead the horses by the reins.

"Jimmy, do you suppose we're going the right way?" Marsha asked. "It doesn't look as if anyone has been through here lately."

"We went straight north, didn't we?" Jimmy asked, pushing aside a branch.

"If this is the right way, I don't see how all the gold panners are going to get through on Sunday," Marsha said with a frown.

"By helicopter, that's how!" Jimmy exclaimed, grabbing Marsha by the arm. He pointed to a clearing up ahead.

Marsha gasped when she saw the helicopter. "Let's tie up the horses here," she said. "They'll make too much noise."

Jimmy and Marsha tied the horses to a tree and crept to the edge of the clearing. They were at the top of a cliff. "Look

"By helicopter, that's how!" Jimmy exclaimed.

over there!" Marsha whispered. "A riverbed!"

"Yeah, a *dry* riverbed!" Jimmy added. Below them to the left was a muddy, old riverbed with a trickle of water running through it.

"So that's the great river of gold!" Marsha said angrily.

"Parker's a big phony, then! And Bradley must be in on it, too!" Jimmy added. "Just let me at them!"

"Shhh," Marsha said. "We've got to be careful."

"You're not going to run away, are you?" Jimmy asked.

"Of course not!" Marsha said in a hurt voice. "I just don't want them to see us, that's all."

"Let's make a dash for that big rock over there, O.K.?" Jimmy asked.

"O.K.," Marsha said. In a few seconds,

31

the two of them were safely hidden behind the rock. From there, they could read the words PARKER GOLD UNLIMITED on the side of the helicopter.

"Hey, look — a cave!" Marsha cried.

"Wow! It must be their hide-out!" Jimmy added.

"Come on, let's go in!" Marsha added.

Marsha and Jimmy crept into the cave on their hands and knees because the opening was so low. After their eyes adjusted to the darkness, they could see a faint light about ten yards away. They moved slowly forward, holding hands so they wouldn't get separated.

When Marsha and Jimmy reached the light, they gasped. In front of them was a regular campsite. It looked as if two men had been sleeping there. The remains of their lunch were spread out on the ground. Nearby was a large map of the surrounding area.

Suddenly, Jimmy and Marsha heard voices at the cave entrance. They ducked behind a stack of boxes in the corner seconds before Parker and Bradley came into the cave.

"Jake, you should have seen the look on the face of this sucker," Ralph was saying. "He fell for the story before I could even finish it. Three thousand bucks! Not bad, eh?"

"Half of that's mine, remember!" Jake said greedily. "How many have we got now?"

"With this Green fellow, we've got the cash down from three families. I'm collecting from five more suckers tomorrow," Ralph boasted.

Marsha and Jimmy looked at each other in disbelief. Ralph was talking about their father!

"Well, speed it up, Ralph. I think the sheriff's getting wise to our game. We've got to clear out by tomorrow night," Jake said. "Now hand over the money."

Ralph took out a wad of bills and handed them to Jake. Jake counted them and stuffed them in a leather pouch. He took a stone out of the cave wall, put the pouch inside, and replaced the stone.

"What do you say we go into town to celebrate?" Jake asked Ralph.

"That's just what I was thinking," Ralph laughed.

As soon as the two men left the cave, Jimmy and Marsha took the leather pouch out of the wall and hurried back to their horses. It was already dark out by the time they reached home.

Quickly, Marsha and Jimmy told their story. Mr. Green called the sheriff,

Ralph took out a wad of bills and handed them to Jake.

and he and his deputy went after the crooks that night. But it was too late. Jake and Ralph were never heard from again.

The nine thousand dollars in the leather pouch was given back to its rightful owners. And Jimmy and Marsha bought fancy new saddles with their reward money.

Doggone It!

Tony Mercer brushed a little sawdust off the oak panel he'd just sanded. He was proud of his woodworking. He'd been working on this chest for a month. Now it was almost done. He just had to join this last panel to the chest and then stain it. Tony looked through his collection of nails, bolts, screws, and pegs for a set of round wooden pegs.

"Wouldn't you know it!" he said, after emptying everything on the basement floor. "I've got dozens of square pegs, but not a single round one! And I was sure I'd have this chest finished today."

Tony looked at his watch. If he hurried, he could make it to the hardware store before it closed. He grabbed his jacket and ran up the stairs two at a time.

"Ginger," he called. His golden retriever puppy bounded after him. Ginger was always happy to go for a ride with Tony.

Together, they jumped into the car and sped toward the hardware store. Ginger stuck her nose out of the window to catch the breeze. She always sat very straight in the seat so she could watch the scenery passing by.

Tony stopped in front of the hardware

Ginger stuck her nose out of the window to catch the breeze.

store. "Hi, Mr. Fields," Tony said. "I need a set of round wooden pegs for my oak chest."

"How's that chest coming along, Tony?" Mr. Fields asked.

"Oh, fine, thanks. I just have to join the last panel to the chest and then stain it," Tony replied.

"Well, that's good to hear. Round wooden pegs, you said? I think I have some in the back," Mr. Fields said. He disappeared into the rear room.

All of a sudden, Tony heard a loud, piercing siren. "Doggone it!" he said, as Mr. Fields came hurrying back to the counter.

"What on earth is that awful noise?" Mr. Fields asked. "It sounds like some kind of alarm."

"Oh, it's just my dog Ginger. When I leave her alone in the car, she gets a bit

"What on earth is that awful noise?"
Mr. Fields asked.

lonely. So she sets off the burglar alarm," Tony explained. "Sometimes, it's really embarrassing."

"Well, I'll be," Mr. Fields chuckled. "That must be a smart dog you've got there."

"Yeah, she's smart all right. But she has to learn that I'm not going to come running every time she pulls one of her tricks."

"Well, I agree with you there, but that noise...!" Mr. Fields said, making a face. "Here are your pegs," he added. He put them on the counter.

"How much do I owe you?" Tony asked.

"Two twenty-five," Mr. Fields said. "I'm giving you a discount. I like to encourage young folks to work with wood. I used to be quite a carpenter myself, you know," he added proudly.

"Yes, I think you mentioned that,"

Tony said politely. He was anxious to get back to the car before Ginger got into any more mischief. "Well, thanks a lot, Mr. Fields," he said, as he laid the money on the counter.

"Give my regards to your parents," Mr. Fields called after Tony.

Tony put the pegs in his jacket pocket and started to cross the street. When he looked toward his car, his mouth dropped open in surprise.

A large crowd was gathered around his car and the car in front of it. There was a police car double-parked next to his car. As he got closer, Tony could see that one police officer was holding down a nasty-looking man. Another officer was handcuffing him. He also noticed that the hood of his car was halfway open.

"Hey, what's going on here?" Tony asked. He pushed his way through the

43

crowd of spectators.

In a few seconds, Tony was standing next to the two police officers. "Will somebody please tell me what's going on?" he asked excitedly.

"You're a lucky young man, mister," one of the officers said to Tony. "This joker here was trying to steal your car battery. But the alarm went off just as we were coming around the corner. It's a good thing, too."

"Yes," the second officer continued, tightening her hold on the car thief. "This creep's known as 'Fingers.' He can hot wire a car in two seconds flat. He has stolen hundreds of cars over the last ten years."

"The only thing he's going to be doing for the next few years is some time in jail," the first officer added. "You're going to have to come down to the station to file a report," he said to Tony.

"Can I stop off at home first?" Tony asked.

"Sure, just come by before ten o'clock tonight. That's when I go off duty. Ask for Officer Jansen, Room 201."

"Fingers" was led to the police car, snarling and cursing under his breath. Then, Tony closed the car hood and got in the car. He forced himself to give Ginger a stern look.

"Ginger, you and I both know that the alarm wasn't set when I went into the hardware store. It can only be set from the inside of the car. So we both know who made it go off."

Tony looked at Ginger's hurt expression and burst into laughter. "But this time, I'm not going to yell at you for setting off the alarm. It was the smartest thing in the world to do! You're a

"You're a genius, Ginger!" Tony exclaimed.

genius, Ginger!" Tony exclaimed, giving his dog a big hug.

"The sky's the limit tonight," he told her. "I'm going to stop at the butcher and pick you up the biggest, juiciest steak you've ever seen!"

Aunt Tessie's Will

Helen Douglas dressed very carefully this morning. She smoothed her hair down and looked at herself in the bedroom mirror. Today was the reading of Great-aunt Tessie's will. Helen was wearing the green wool dress that Tessie had given her two winters ago.

"It brings out the fire in your hair," Tessie had said when Helen first tried on the dress. Helen had thick, golden-red hair that reached to her waist. Tessie used to have hair just like that when she was young. But over the years, her red hair had turned gray. She wore her thick, silvery hair in a bun until her death at age ninety-three.

Helen got a lump in her throat when she thought about her great-aunt. *Tessie was a truly grand lady,* she thought. Some people said Tessie wasn't quite right in the mind the last few years of her life. Helen knew better. Tessie had only pretended to be a little crazy. That way, people would leave her alone. Tessie liked to live alone with her memories in her dusty, old house that was filled with antiques. She wore dresses that were in style fifty years

*Helen was wearing the green wool dress
that Tessie had given her two winters ago.*

ago. She never owned a TV or a radio.

Helen was one of the very few people Tessie trusted. She used to spend long afternoons with her great-aunt, listening to Tessie's wonderful stories from the past. Helen and Tessie understood each other.

"Come on, Helen. It's time to go," Helen's mother said, poking her head into the room.

Helen blinked back her tears and picked up her purse. "How do I look?" she asked her mother.

"Beautiful, dear. That was Tessie's favorite dress, wasn't it?" Mrs. Douglas asked gently, putting her arm around Helen.

Helen was very quiet on the way to the reading. She felt sad but excited at the same time. Tessie had told Helen she was leaving everything to her.

Helen wondered what "everything" would be. Some people said Tessie was a wealthy woman. No one really knew for sure. Tessie had kept the truth to herself. She loved secrets.

The reading was at Great-aunt Tessie's quaint old house. There were only a few friends and relatives there. They greeted each other. Then they settled down to listen to Mr. Ramsey, the lawyer.

"As you know," Mr. Ramsey began, "we are gathered here today for the reading of Teresa Mae Gardiner's will. First, Mrs. Gardiner requested that this house be left exactly as it is. She wanted it to be a museum showing American life at the turn of this century."

"What a nice idea," Helen whispered to her mother.

"Second, she requested that all of her

stocks and bonds go to Joseph Armour," Mr. Ramsey continued.

A gasp went through the room.

"Who's *that*?" Mrs. Douglas asked angrily.

"That's me, ma'am," said a round man with a fringe of white hair. Helen recognized him—he was Tessie's next-door neighbor. Tessie once told Helen that she didn't trust Mr. Armour because he was always poking his nose into other people's business.

That's very strange, Helen thought to herself. *Why would Tessie leave it all to him?*

"There must be some mistake," Mr. Douglas said to Mr. Ramsey. "Tessie showed me her will a few years ago. It clearly stated that everything was to be left to my daughter, Helen Douglas."

"I'm sorry, Mr. Douglas," Mr. Ramsey

replied, "but there's no mistake. Mrs. Gardiner changed her will shortly before she died. Now please let me finish."

Mr. Douglas sank back in his seat. His eyes were flashing angrily. He looked at Mrs. Douglas. She seemed as upset as he was. Helen looked stunned and hurt.

Mr. Ramsey cleared his throat. "Finally, Mrs. Gardiner requested that all her personal belongings be given to her great-niece, Helen Douglas. This includes all clothing, jewelry, and books, as well as Mrs. Gardiner's antique doll collection." Mr. Ramsey took off his glasses and looked at the group. "That concludes the reading of the will of Teresa Mae Gardiner," he said.

That night after dinner, Helen and her parents sat up late. They were discussing the events of the day.

Mr. Ramsey took off his glasses and looked at the group.

"The strangest part is that Tessie never trusted Mr. Armour. She told me so herself!" Helen said.

"That Armour is a crook!" Mr. Douglas exclaimed. "Somehow, he must have gotten his hands on her will and changed it without Tessie finding out."

"But how?" Mrs. Douglas asked. "Tessie kept the will locked in her bank vault."

"I just don't know," Mr. Douglas sighed. "But I think we should have another lawyer take a look at the will."

"Mom," Helen said thoughtfully, "will you give me a ride to Tessie's house tomorrow?"

"Why certainly, dear," Mrs. Douglas replied. "Is there any special reason?"

"I just want to take a last look around," Helen said quietly.

The next morning, Mrs. Douglas

dropped Helen at Tessie's. "I'll pick you up at noon, O.K.?" she asked Helen.

"O.K.," Helen replied. "And thanks a lot, Mom."

Helen entered Tessie's house and locked the door behind her. She went directly to Tessie's bedroom. A beautiful china doll with a pink satin dress, a ruffled petticoat, and tiny pink slippers sat on top of Tessie's dresser.

Helen reached inside the petticoat and pulled out a tiny golden key. Then she took down the old-fashioned portrait of Tessie that hung over the bed. She pressed a certain spot on the wall and a hidden panel swung around. On the back of the panel was a door with a little keyhole.

Helen unlocked the door with the golden key and took out Tessie's diaries. There were four thick volumes with

*Helen unlocked the door with the golden key
and took out Tessie's diaries.*

pearly covers, tied together with a blue satin ribbon. Helen was the only one in the world who knew about these diaries. Tessie used to read from them once in a great while. Now these diaries belonged to Helen!

Helen locked the bedroom door and hugged the diaries tightly. She had two whole hours to look through them! She flipped to the last entry. It was dated only one week before Tessie's death.

That night at dinner, Helen and her mother and her father all started to talk at once.

"Hold on a minute!" Mr. Douglas said. "Go ahead, Helen, you seem ready to burst with excitement," he added.

Helen could barely sit in her seat. "Oh, Daddy, you were right about Mr. Armour!" she exclaimed. "I looked at Aunt Tessie's diary today. Only a week before she died, Mr. Armour visited her. He convinced her that her will might not be valid because it was written so many years ago. He said the laws had changed recently. He used to be a lawyer himself, so Tessie believed him. She had him fetch the will out of her vault. He went over it with her. He said it was O.K. after all and returned it to the bank vault."

"Making a few little changes on the way to the bank, no doubt!" Mr. Douglas said grimly. "My news makes matters even worse, I'm afraid. I had the top lawyer in town look over the will this afternoon. It's all in perfect order. Whoever wrote it did a flawless job. There's nothing we can do about it!"

"Would you two please let me tell you the good news now?" Mrs. Douglas asked with a twinkle in her eyes.

"What is it?" Helen and her father

nearly shouted.

"I just spoke with Mr. Ramsey on the telephone. He said that all of Tessie's stocks and bonds are worthless! Tessie put all her money into a toy company that went bankrupt ten years ago. Of course, you know Tessie – she never told anyone about this. She just held on to the stock all these years."

"So much for Mr. Armour's fortune!" Mr. Douglas snorted.

"Aunt Tessie always did love surprising people!" Helen said with a smile.

Break-In

Eddie Nelson adjusted the picture on his parents' TV. Then he stuffed two pillows behind his head so that he could see better. He lay back and let his thoughts wander.

"This is the life!" he said to his friend, Bob Gunther. Bob was making ham and cheese sandwiches on the Nelsons' best

*Bob was making ham and cheese sandwiches
on the Nelsons' best sofa.*

sofa. "Just think," Eddie continued, "I'd be in English right now. And Mrs. Thomas would be asking me for my paper on Mark Twain—which I haven't even started yet."

"Aw, Eddie, I thought we agreed not to talk about school today. I mean, what's the use of cutting if you spend all day talking about school?"

"Yeah, I guess you're right," Eddie said. "How about passing me a soda?"

"Just a minute. Can't you see I'm busy?" Bob grunted under his breath. He was trying to smear mustard on all four sandwiches at once.

"I can see you're making a mess of the sofa, you slob! You got mustard all over the cushion."

"I was doing fine till you interrupted me," Bob replied. "Besides, it wipes right off, see?" As Bob spoke, he tried to wipe the mustard off with a napkin. Instead, he spread it onto the other cushion.

"Hey, stop! You're just making it worse!" Eddie shouted. He grabbed Bob's napkin. "Let's eat, already. I'll clean this up later."

Bob gave Eddie two huge sandwiches, a bag of potato chips, and a soda.

Eddie raised his soda in the air. "Three cheers for the cook! Hip, hip, hooray! Hip, hip, hooray! Hip, hip—"

Bob put his hand over Eddie's mouth. "Shhh! Don't say a word," he whispered.

Eddie scowled and tried to figure out what Bob was doing. He seemed to be listening for something.

Suddenly, the boys heard a soft tapping coming from downstairs. "It sounds as if it's coming from the dining room," Eddie whispered.

"Could it be your mom?" Bob asked.

"No, she won't be back before six," Eddie said as the tapping got louder and louder.

"This is serious. Look for something we can use as a weapon," Bob said, opening every drawer in sight.

"Shhh," Eddie said, "stop that. I have an idea." Eddie opened his parents' large walk-in closet and went inside. When he came out, he was carrying a bright red fire extinguisher.

"Holy smokes!" Bob exclaimed. "Where on earth did that come from?"

"My dad's a safety nut," Eddie said. "He bought five of these for the house. Sometimes we even have fire drills with the whole family!"

Just as Bob opened his mouth to speak, the tapping suddenly ended with a huge crash. Somebody had broken through the plate-glass window in the dining room!

"You call the police!" Eddie whispered. "I'll stand guard by the door." Eddie's heart was pounding. He could hear heavy footsteps thudding through the living room. Then — he could hardly believe his ears — the footsteps headed for the stairway!

The boys were in the first room to the right at the top of the stairs. Bob grabbed a flowerpot and joined Eddie behind the half-open door. They were determined to take the burglar by surprise.

Eddie gripped the fire extinguisher tightly in both hands. The footsteps reached the top of the stairs, and then there was silence. Eddie was afraid the burglar could hear his heart beating. He felt like screaming.

Finally, the footsteps moved slowly to the left. That was the bathroom.

Again they stopped. Bob felt sweat running down his back. He had a terrible itch on his left knee. But he didn't move a muscle.

The boys looked at each other. This was it! The footsteps were moving straight toward the boys' hiding place now. In a flash, Eddie sprayed the burglar in the face while Bob hit him over the head with the flowerpot. The burglar was surprised, all right—and out cold! The boys stared at the man, but they couldn't see his face because of all the foam covering it.

"No gun!" Eddie exclaimed. He was disappointed.

"Hey, look at this!" Bob said, pointing to a long, curved knife on the floor. He took off one of his socks and placed it on his hand. Then he picked the knife up very carefully.

*Eddie sprayed the burglar in the face while
Bob hit him over the head with the flowerpot.*

"Fingerprints, you know," he explained to Eddie.

"Are you boys all right?" a gruff voice asked.

The boys turned around to face a police sergeant and another officer.

"Are we all right? We're great!" Eddie boasted. "Look!" He pointed to the burglar.

"Yeah, we got this creep all by ourselves! Hey, we're heroes!" Bob added.

"You certainly are!" the sergeant said with a big smile. He bent down and wiped some of the foam off the burglar's face. "Do you know who this 'creep' is?"

Eddie and Bob stared at the burglar and stepped back a few inches.

"No, but he sure looks ugly," Eddie said.

"And mean, too. Is he famous?" Bob asked.

"In a manner of speaking," the sergeant said with a twinkle in his eye. He handcuffed the burglar as he spoke. "This man has robbed everything from banks to pizza parlors to little old ladies. He's been in and out of jail all his life. He keeps on escaping. That's why they call him Slippery Sal."

"I read about him in the paper!" Bob said proudly. "He *is* famous!"

"Is there a reward for catching him?" Eddie askod.

"There certainly is . . . one thousand dollars!" the sergeant replied. "But we'll straighten all that out later. You boys will have to come down to the station and answer some questions. But first, do you mind telling me where your phone is?"

The next day, the whole school was buzzing with the news about Slippery

Bob and Eddie were heroes.

Sal. Bob and Eddie were heroes. All the kids followed them down the hall, asking them to repeat their story. As for Bob and Eddie, they loved all the attention. Eddie's English teacher didn't even yell at him about the paper on Mark Twain.

At 1:30, Eddie was called down to the principal's office. When he got there, he saw Bob sitting inside.

They must be giving us some kind of award, he thought to himself. He gave Bob a wink.

"Well, boys," the principal began, "that was quite an adventure you had yesterday. We're all very proud of the way you captured that escaped criminal." She paused and the smile left her face. "However, heroes or not, you still have to obey the rules of this school, the same as all our other students. The fact

73

of the matter is, you boys were cutting school yesterday. You know what the penalty for that is." Again, the principal paused and looked sternly at the two boys. "Both of you are to report to detention hall at 3:00 P.M. today."

Bob and Eddie looked at each other in shock. Detention hall! Them?

"Mrs. Winthrop will be expecting you. Is that clear?"

"Yes, ma'am," the boys muttered.

"That will be all."

Oil Job

Tim Weston turned north on Elm Street. His old car began to make strange noises. It coughed and snorted and backfired a few times. Then it came to a dead stop in front of Bobby's Hobby Shop.

"Come on, Pudgy, don't die on me now," he pleaded. Tim jiggled the key in the ignition. He banged a certain spot on the dashboard, and put the car into neutral. Again, he tried to start the car.

"This must be serious," Tim muttered, making a face. "I don't understand it! If it were a loose connection, she would have shown at least some signs of life."

Tim sniffed and then frowned. There was a strong smell of oil. He jumped out of the car and opened the hood. The oil was really low. Then he looked under the car. Tim could see a small, shiny pool of black liquid. "Another leak," he frowned. "This just isn't my day."

He straightened up and sighed. *If I can just get enough oil in Pudgy to make it home, I can patch up that leak tonight,* he thought. There was a gas station at the end of the block.

Tim bought a quart of oil. He started back to the car. He passed by the bakery and was approaching the bank. As he glanced in the bank window, he looked again. A bank holdup seemed to be in progress!

Tim pressed his face to the glass to get a better look. But he quickly ducked down. One of the two bank robbers had turned in his direction. A shot tore through the plate-glass window where Tim's face had been.

"Holy smokes!" Tim gulped. "That was a close call!" His heart was pounding, but he was thinking clearly. He had an idea. Tim opened the oil can with shaking hands. He threw the oil across the sidewalk in front of the doors to the bank. He crouched behind a nearby bush just as two robbers burst through the doors.

The first robber was a small man. He hit the oil and went sliding toward the

*The first robber hit the oil and went
sliding toward the curb.*

curb, shouting and waving his arms wildly. Before he could regain his balance, the second robber, a bigger man, came crashing into the first robber. He knocked him over. Both men dropped their guns in the fall.

Tim could hear a police siren very close by. He had squeezed himself into a little ball and hidden behind a bush. Now, he hoped that the robbers wouldn't notice him. As he peeked through an opening in the bush, the big, ugly looking robber was struggling to get up. The little robber seemed to be out cold.

As the big man got to his feet and reached for his gun, a voice came over a loudspeaker: *"Drop it right there or we'll shoot! Give up—you're surrounded!"*

Tim strained to see through the bush. He didn't dare stand up, although his back was hurting him from sitting in such an uncomfortable position. But he could tell that the big, rough-looking robber was the one who had shot at him from inside the bank.

The big robber put up his hands when he saw the two squad cars full of police. His face was purple with rage. He seemed to be looking for someone. Tim's heart skipped a beat, and he sunk even lower toward the ground.

The big robber turned toward Tim, growling in anger. Tim couldn't hear what he was saying, but he was greatly relieved when two police officers handcuffed the big robber. They led him off to one of the squad cars.

The little robber had come to, but he was still very groggy. He was handcuffed and half-carried to a second squad car.

Now, Tim finally felt safe. He stood

*The big robber put up his hands when he saw
the two squad cars full of police.*

up and came out from behind the bush. He stretched his cramped muscles. He brushed the dirt off his shirt and pants.

"Whew," he sighed as he watched the squad cars drive away. "What a day this has been!" He wiped the sweat off his forehead and looked at the empty oil can. *Just think — this all happened because old Pudgy sprang a leak on me,* he thought.

Tim headed back toward the gas station. *No one's going to believe me when I tell them about the oil job those two just got!*

The Wall of Ice

The group of hikers paused when they reached flat ground. They stood on a narrow shelf overlooking the Taminaw Valley. It was nearly noon now, and they'd been climbing since sunrise. If all went well, they would reach the top of Mount Healy in a couple of hours.

"Hey, Dale, come over here! You've got to see this view!" Linda Cartwright said to her brother.

"All right, all right, I'll be there in a minute," Dale said. He was trying to find something in his backpack. "Aha!" he exclaimed, pulling out a peanut-butter-and-jelly sandwich. He took a gigantic bite of the sandwich and joined his sister.

The Taminaw Valley spread out before them. Its square fields were green and yellow and dotted with farmhouses.

"We're really lucky to have such a clear day," Dale said. He pointed to the west. "Look! You can see Arrow Lake from here, and that's forty miles away!"

Peter O'Keefe walked over to the Cartwrights. Peter was the leader of the hiking group. "It's time we moved on," he said. "We don't want to get caught on

The group of hikers paused when they reached flat ground.

the mountain at dusk." He called to the other two hikers, Wendy Reeve and Mark Daniels.

Soon, the group was on its way again. As the hikers climbed, the trees thinned out. The upper part of the mountain was rocky and covered with snow. The hikers panted as they made their way up the steep, slippery slope.

As the group climbed, clouds began to gather. A sharp wind made the hikers shiver and snow began to fall. They pulled their coat collars up and wrapped scarves around their faces.

"Ouch!" Wendy exclaimed, holding her cheek. The tiny pieces of ice and snow felt like razors as they blew in her face.

"Keep your head low, like this," Peter said. He bent over so that the top of his head faced forward. He was worried. It looked as if they were headed for a bad ice storm.

"We're almost at the top," he said to the others. "Just hang in there for a few more minutes!" His words were carried away on the wind. It was no use trying to talk right now.

The group pushed on, their faces red and sore from the wet and cold. They dug their metal picks into the ground to keep from slipping.

They had climbed over a mile when, suddenly, Peter shouted and raised his arms. No one could understand what he was saying. As the four hikers gathered around Peter, he pointed toward something. The snow cleared away for a moment and the group began to cheer. Just ahead were an American flag and a little hut. They were at the top of the mountain!

The hikers stood next to the hut and

*Just ahead were an American flag and
a little hut.*

tried to look out over the valley. But the snow was blowing worse than before. They couldn't see more than a few feet in front of them.

Mark was the most disappointed. He was a photographer, and he'd hoped to get some great shots from the top of Mount Healy.

"Can't we wait a while to see if it clears up?" he asked miserably.

"No, Mark. I'm afraid this storm isn't going to let up for hours," Peter said. "We've got to get back as soon as possible. The slopes are being coated with ice."

Indeed, the snow had turned to icy sleet. The sky was getting darker by the minute. It was going to be a rough descent. The ground was icy and the wind was biting cold.

The hikers pulled their scarves up

around their faces. Peter tied them all together with a long rope so that nobody would get lost. The storm was so fierce, they couldn't see more than a few feet ahead of them.

Peter led the way. He had climbed this mountain so many times he knew it very well. It was a good thing, because not a landmark could be seen now. Peter had a compass, but mostly he made his way by pure instinct.

Suddenly, he stopped and listened intently. "Quick, get back! Duck down!" he yelled, pushing the group under a rocky ledge.

The hikers heard a rumbling sound above them. It grew louder and louder, until it became a roar. The hikers hugged the ground, hardly daring to breathe. Huge boulders of ice and snow tumbled down the mountain, leveling everything in their path. They roared by the exact spot where the group had been standing.

Linda clutched her brother tightly. Mark and Wendy huddled against the snowy ledge, speechless. Peter was relieved that he'd heard that distant rumble in time. His hands shook as he thought of their narrow escape.

He turned to the group. "Are you all O.K.?" The others nodded. They were badly shaken, but no one was hurt.

"We've all had a bad scare, but it's over now. We've got to pull ourselves together and get out of here," Peter said gently. "Listen carefully. We're going to have to take a different route down. The boulders have blocked our way. Even if we could get around them, it would be too risky. More may fall any time now. The path we're taking is very steep. I know you can all do it if you just stay calm and follow instructions."

The group followed Peter without a word. The snow had let up slightly. They made their way west across a narrow pass. Soon, they reached a cliff overlooking a steep wall of ice. The wall dropped almost straight down for sixty feet.

Peter took out a heavy rope and tied it around a huge rock.

"This looks like a dead end," Mark said.

Linda's eyes opened wide as she realized what Peter was doing. "Do you expect us to go down *there*?" she asked, pointing to the wall of ice.

"Even a mountain goat couldn't climb down that thing!" Wendy added.

"We're not climbing down," Peter said. "We're *sliding* down."

"I think when I get home, I'm going to

stick to nice, safe sports — like football," Dale said. His laugh sounded forced.

Dale was the first to go down. With one end of the rope around the rock and the other end around his waist, he pushed off. He slid down the wall of ice on his back, as Peter instructed. When he reached the bottom, he untied the rope and signaled that he was O.K.

Linda, Mark, and Wendy followed the same way, with Peter's help. At last, it was Peter's turn. He tied the rope around his waist and pushed off. When he was halfway down, he heard a loud rumbling. A huge boulder roared down the mountain. It hit the rock holding the rope and shattered it to pieces.

Peter was showered with stones as the rope gave way. The others watched in horror as he started to fall. It was at least a thirty-foot drop to the sharp and jagged rocks below.

Peter managed to clutch a small ledge in the wall, about fifteen feet off the ground. As he dangled in midair, his grasp weakened. He was dazed, and his head was bleeding from the stone shower.

Someone had an idea. In a flash, rocks were stacked up against the wall. Mark stood on top of the rocks, and Dale climbed on his shoulders. Dale grabbed Peter's leg just as Peter's grip loosened. With Wendy and Linda's help, Dale eased Peter to the ground.

They all looked at Peter anxiously. His eyes were closed, and he looked deathly pale. Linda cleaned the blood off his forehead with snow. Mark held a water canteen to his lips.

Peter opened his eyes and looked at the group.

"Say something, Peter. Are you all

Mark stood on top of the rocks, and Dale climbed on his shoulders.

right?" Wendy asked tearfully.

"I think so," Peter said slowly. The others helped him to his feet. He groaned as he straightened up. "It's nothing that a hot bath and a good night's rest won't cure," he said.

Soon, the group was on its way again. The rest of the descent was much easier. By nightfall, the hikers reached the foot of Mount Healy. They had made it!